JANET S. WONG

PICTURES BY
Margaret Chodos-Irvine

VOYAGER BOOKS
HARCOURT, INC.

Orlando Austin New York San Diego Toronto London

Seven days a week,
fifty-two weeks,
three hundred sixty-four days a year
(and three hundred sixty-five in a leap year),
our store is open.

Christmas is the only day we close.

Even on Thanksgiving we open the store.
Even on New Year's Day.
Even today, the Fourth of July.

I hear the parade coming this way—
boom, boom, boom.

I smell apple pie
in Laura's oven upstairs
and—

chow mein in our kitchen.
Chow mein!
Chinese food on the Fourth of July?

No one wants Chinese food
on the Fourth of July, I say.

Fireworks are Chinese, Father says,
and hands me a pan full of sweet-and-sour pork.

I hear the parade—

BOOM, BOOM, BOOM.

I hear the parade passing by.

Noon, and customers come
for soda and potato chips.

One o'clock,
and they buy ice cream.

Two o'clock.
The egg rolls are getting hard.

Four o'clock,
and the noodles feel like shoelaces.

Three o'clock.
Ice and matches.

No one wants Chinese food on the Fourth of July, I say.
Mother piles noodles on my plate.

My parents do not understand all American things.
They were not born here.

Even though my father has lived here
since he was twelve,
even though my mother loves apple pie,
I cannot expect them to know
                              Americans
do not eat Chinese food
on the Fourth of July.

So, I straighten the milk and the videos
and sample a few new candy bars

until five o'clock,

when two hungry customers walk inside
for some Chinese food to go.

I tell them no one—no one—came,
so we ate it up ourselves

but they smell food in the kitchen
now—

and Mother walks through the swinging door
holding a tray of chicken chow mein,

and Father follows her step for step
with a brand-new pan of sweet-and-sour pork—

and three more people get in line,
eleven more at six o'clock,
nine at seven,
twelve by eight,

more and more and more and more

until it's time to close the store—

time to climb to our rooftop chairs,
way up high, beyond the crowd,

where we sit and watch the fireworks show—

and eat
our apple pie.

www.HarcourtBooks.com

First Voyager Books edition 2006

Voyager Books is a trademark of Harcourt, Inc., registered in the United States of America and/or other jurisdictions.

The Library of Congress has cataloged the hardcover edition as follows:
Wong, Janet S.
Apple pie Fourth of July/by Janet S. Wong; illustrated by Margaret Chodos-Irvine.
p. cm.
Summary: A Chinese American child fears that the food her parents are preparing to sell on the Fourth of July will not be eaten.
[1. Fourth of July—Fiction.   2. Cookery, Chinese—Fiction.   3. Chinese Americans—Fiction.]
I. Chodos-Irvine, Margaret, ill.   II. Title.   PZ7.W842115Ap   2002
[E]—dc21   2001001313
ISBN-13: 978-0152-02543-4   ISBN-10: 0-15-202543-X
ISBN-13: 978-0152-05708-4 pb   ISBN-10: 0-15-205708-0 pb

LEO   10 9 8 7 6
4500331519

The illustrations in this book were created using a variety of printmaking techniques on Lana printmaking paper.
The display lettering was created by Margaret Chodos-Irvine and Judythe Sieck.
The text type was set in Stone Sans Bold.
Color separations by Bright Arts Ltd., Hong Kong
Printed and bound by LEO, China
Production supervision by Pascha Gerlinger
Designed by Margaret Chodos-Irvine and Judythe Sieck

To Jeannette Larson, whose warmth and humor
made this story come alive
—J. S. W.

To Marty and Rosalyn Chodos, for nurturing
my creative inclinations
—M. C.-I.